To Seth Caine
who helped me find my wings
J.D.
~
For Greta
my baby bird
R.A.

First published 1998 by Walker Books Ltd
87 Vauxhall Walk, London SE11 5HJ

10 9 8 7 6 5 4 3 2 1

Text © 1998 Joyce Dunbar
Illustrations © 1998 Russell Ayto

The right of Joyce Dunbar
to be identified as author
of this work has been asserted
by her in accordance
with the Copyright, Designs
and Patents Act 1988.

This book has been
typeset in Journal Text.
Printed in Italy

British Library Cataloguing
in Publication Data
A catalogue record
for this book is available
from the British Library.

ISBN 0-7445-4921-3

Baby Bird

written by

Joyce Dunbar

illustrated by

Russell Ayto

WALKER BOOKS

AND SUBSIDIARIES

LONDON · BOSTON · SYDNEY

This is the bird that

climbed out of the nest and ...

flop

flop

flop

... he fell!

This is the squirrel that

sniffed at the bird that fell.

This is the bee that

BIZZ

buzzed round the bird that fell.

This is the frog that

hopped over the bird that fell.

This is the cat that

stalked the bird ...

and fell himself

(which was just as well).

This is the dog that opened wide

and a bird that nearly walked inside.

A baby bird that wanted to fly

up, up above, up above in the sky ...

and thought he would have

just one more try ...

flap

flap

flap

flap   flap   flap...

This is the bird

that flew!

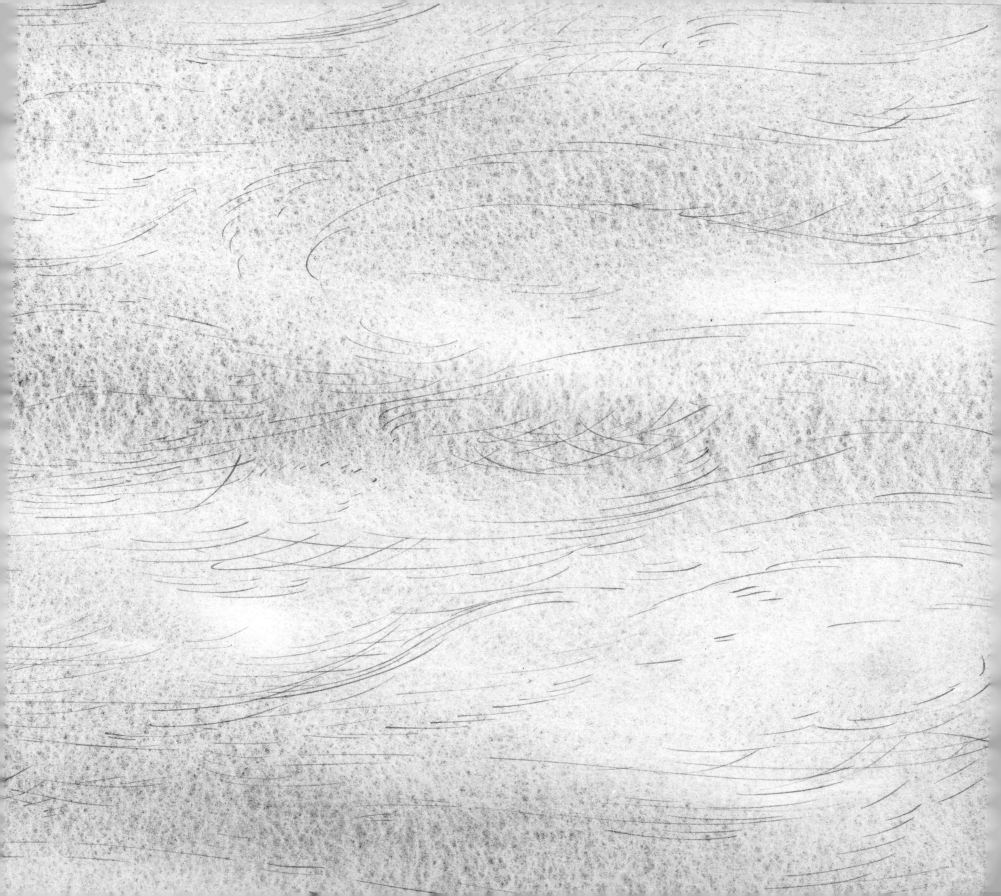